Party of Sweet Foursome

Bisexual Menage Erotic Short Story

Contents

Chapter 1 1

Chapter 2 7

Chapter 3 12

Chapter 4 18

Epilogue 27

Chapter 1

Ruby met Jason three years ago back when she was a girl chasing for what seemed an impossible dream, with three jobs and living on a house that didn't feel like home. Trying to get out as soon as possible but no matter how many universities she applied to for a scholarship they all came declined, she needed to live a little, but how could she? If she was basically working all day long, trying to support her little sisters and saving so she could move out and start her career? What chance did she have to live? That wasn't living.

Her schedule was to wake up go to work and go back home to sleep, seven days a week for almost 3 complete years. No time for dating not boys or girls. She only had eyes for her long-term goal and getting the hell out of her "Home" as soon as she could.

High school had been a wild place for Ruby, from hooking up with the football team players and some cheerleaders she had a crazy last 2 years. Not that she was that type of girl anymore. But she didn't put a label to her sexuality not to who she felt attracted to, if she felt the connection, she was up for it. And to her there wasn't anything more beautiful than a fluid sexuality.

Nowadays it was difficult and rare for her to hook up with girls or even boys with her full-time schedule. She barely had time for a quick on a car before heading home and it was too uncomfortable, that's what she said to herself when she found herself on the back seat of a pickup truck three weeks ago with a guy she met on tinder. He said he was going to go and meet her at her job and then they would do something, but that something ended up being a quickie of 10 minutes on his backseat. Rough, dry, and selfish quickie.

Now Jason was a regular at the bar Ruby works during weekends, he was a good-looking guy. Relatively long hair, nice trimmed beard, and always walked with a confident flow that made anyone look on his way. Ruby wasn't attracted to his type; all pretentious snob looking guy, but there was something about him. There was more under the layers that he so proudly displayed around, what caught Ruby's attention was that he came with mixed groups, and most of the time he had a different partner, sometimes a girl, but other times a boy. He always ordered the same, first a Gin tonic for him and usually a Vodka soda for his partner. Then a bottle of champagne or wine depending if he was in a group or alone and then he would whisper something on his or her ear and they would leave. He always left Ruby good tips, which she appreciated.

But who was this guy with this confidence, doing whomever he pleased? More than once he looked in her direction and smiled at her. Ruby always responded back with her best smile, but it never went more than that. No sentences were exchanged.

Until one night he showed up alone, no group, no partner, just himself. He sat on the bar and Ruby served him his gin tonic before he even asked for it.

"You know me well," he took a sip of his drink and his eyes glowed. "Handy girl," He looked at her and they both smiled. That was the beginning.

He kept coming to the bar from time to time, sometimes alone sometimes with company and he always sat with her, when he was alone. And when he wasn't too fond of his companion, he dismissed them and joined Ruby at the bar, until the end of her shift.

She joined him for a drink asking for a negroni, "good taste" Jason said raising his glass.

"For an interesting friendship," their glasses clinked and they chatter for hours before leaving.

Later that night before closing Ruby walked to the bathroom, Jason was still there, he had been at the bar talking and drinking for the past 2 hours. She needed to make sure her face was decent at least. She was about to close the door when Jason entered and shut it down behind him

"…You are not supposed to—"

He shushed her by kissing her and firmly grabbed her
ass while doing so. She moaned in his mouth and he
savored her, he tasted of gin and something else. He
kissed her neck, and bit her earlobe. Ruby moaned
and he slide his hand on her pants, touching her front,
she was a little guarded, she hadn't had much action
recently. "Vintage," he laughed and grabbed Ruby's
breast with one hand as he touched all over her with
another, he kept kissing her neck and Ruby felt
heating up inside with his arousal.

Ruby felt his hardness on her back, she pressed
against it making him moan. "Ahh easy girl," as he
kept playing with her clitoris going in slow circles,
making her moan.

"I want you to cum for me, would you do that?" She
nodded and bit on his arm as he increased the speed
and kissed her desperately. Working his fingers Jason
pushed with deep and slow strokes, he kept pinching
her nipples, giving her a tingling sensation in her wet
clit.

"Keep going" she gasped as he played with her
breasts and box. Slowly entering and then playing
around, she still had her pants on and he was also
fully dressed, he was hard but hadn't even touched
himself, he was just trying to please her.

"Oh… my," Ruby started to moan, luckily the music was loud enough that no one should hear her, "Yes, yes!" she begged him to continue.

Ruby heard the zipper open and without a word Jason pressed the tip of his cock against her.
"Please, just fuck me," Ruby shouted impatiently.

He leaned forward, lifting her slightly against the wall and thrust in. Seduced by the tight lips swallowing his cock, Jason quickly started to push against her with force. Pushing her against the wall, Jason groaned and rocked his dick in and out of Ruby. Blow after blow she felt his hard dick caress her dripping pussy, until she was gasping for air as she reached her climax with her pants still on, making her pants a warm mess. Immediately after she felt Jason pull out, followed by a loud groan he unloaded into her pants.

"Tasty" he said as he licked his fingers and she felt her body shiver inside out.

"Come, I'll take you home," She left thought the back door and he was there waiting for her, she still had some cum on her pants, that was something that was supposed to happen to guys only, not her. But damn it felt hot, she felt relaxed and different at the same time. The ride home was silent compared to their chatter the whole night, "This is me, thanks for the ride, I had a really good time," Jason gazed at her for a moment. "So did I, hand me your phone". She did as he asked and Jason added his number. "Text me tomorrow, there is a place I would like to take you to if you are up for an adventure."

"Sure, tomorrow then," he pressed a soft kiss on her lips before she got out of his car and entered her house. That night it took her lot of effort to fall asleep as her mind went around what had happened that night. Had he been giving her signals and she was that desperate and blind to follow? He was a player and she knew that. But a player could be played, right?

Chapter 2

That night Ruby thought she was going to struggle to sleep after such a long week of work, but once she got out of a nice warm shower, washing the mess she was in and checked with her co-worker to change their shift for this weekend, she slept like a baby. Could be that the release had in fact helped her.

Ruby texted him after she had shaved her legs, armpits, and intimate areas, cleaned her eyebrows, did a facial, washer her hair and painted her nails feet and hands, something she had not done for ages. He replied within a couple of minutes. *"Hey Scarlet,"* he mocked, he must have known her name was Ruby, didn't he?

"Ruby here, just checking in." She started to get anxious as the bubbles showed up and disappear under his name. *"We are going to an adult-exclusive party, you are going to be my plus one, dress nicely. There will be potential suitors for both of us, are you in?"* Ruby started to take in all he said and understood what type of party this was, it wasn't just an adult party it was more than that, she had heard rumors about people having these types of parties, couples basically. *"Yes, where do I meet you?"* She replied and he sent her his address telling to meet at his place so they could pre-game and leave together.

She sorted out her top 3 outfits, she could wear a black, yellow, or red dress, her hair was already red. So, wearing something red was a hard no, instead, she tried on her black dress, her boobs look bigger on them and she looked pale, she liked how it fit, making her waist look extra slim and was just 2 inches above her knees. Sensual but not too slutty, a short kinda dress. She let her hair bounce in a nice flow, painted her lips with her Ruby Woo a perfect red that matched her hair, went well with her skin, and complimented her name.

She was too nervous to eat anything, she managed to eat a salad before leaving, walking back to the bathroom brushing her teeth, making sure her makeup was on point and still looking soft and natural, she didn't want to look too girlish she was going for the more mature look. And this dress with the right lipstick made it look bomb.

Black high heels and her evening bag. She called a taxi, her mother gave her disapproval looks as she waited at the front door, but she left without saying anything, her little sister told she look cute and that was the acceptance she needed, it gave her a big smile, she kissed her on the cheeks, leaving a red mark there.

Ruby arrived at a fancy looking condo she waited at the lobby for Jason's confirmation before she was let in. He opened the door and was waiting for her shirtless, he was wearing a pair of dark blue pants and brown shoes. His chest was mid hairy, in the right areas and he was in great shape, his apartment looked like a magazine picture.

Everything was well thought, every furniture, every ornament, every last detail, it all worked in harmony it felt peaceful and beautiful. Such an elegant but weird looking apartment but somehow it was exactly what she had imagined. "Who are you?" Ruby mentioned as she walked to the living room finding a big piano and frames hanging from the wall. "Jason and you are.. Ruby?" He said sarcastically.

Ruby exhaled rolling her eyes and said "I meant what do you do, are you a designer or something like that?"

"No not really, I'm an editor, it pays well and I have a friend who is an interior designer and helped me to get this place all cozy and with just the correct vibe if you will." He handed Ruby a glass of wine and they sat on a small bar he had in the living room, "Want me to play something?" He said as he sat on the piano and played a slow lullaby, he looked like a model on a front page, shirtless, build guy, a glass of wine next to him, and playing on the piano in a nice-looking apartment? Ruby was waiting for someone pinch her.

" Um, yes, I can feel the positive vibe," she said taking a sip of her glass as she looked around.

"Who do you live with Ruby?"

She stopped for a moment before saying something stupid, "With my parents, but I'm trying to start college again, move somewhere else. Live, but in order to get into a school they tell me I need to live first, so… I'm struggling." I felt like a fraud, I just wanted to sink in this chair right here and right now.

"Not everyone has it clear, that just means you are not someone who goes for the easy or simple road and I can appreciate that, "Jason said.

Somehow having a stranger praising her for her lack of decision comforted her in a really nice way, looking at his point of view it made sense. She was really thinking it though before making a decision, or maybe he was just being polite.

He stood up doing a dorky dance as he took a gray plain shirt hanging next to the piano. "Are you ready to start living Scarlet?" he took his keys and walked to the elevator.

"Can anyone be ready for that?"

He walked out grabbed his keys and she followed.

"You are right, maybe no one truly is."

"Have you been to a swing meeting party?" His voice echoed on the elevator.

"No, but I think I have an idea."

"Be safe, have fun and beware of the wolves." He gave me a broad smile as we walk in an elevator that took us to a gigantic penthouse full of beautiful people sharing drinks and talking. The room was long and the other side was purely made of glass with an open view to the nighttime city. This was definitely paradise for bisexuals.

Someone passed around a tray with glass filled with some rose liquid, champagne? Wine? I couldn't tell, Jason grabbed two glasses and handed one to me. "Welcome to paradise Mademoiselle."

Chapter 3

I looked around taking in every space, every person, every smile, everyone was having a good time. Jason went to greet someone and I was by myself for, not for too long as a young petite girl approached me with a big smile on her face. "I guess you are new here, Alyssa, nice to meet you,"

I shook her hand and she held onto mine. "Ruby, likewise" she giggled.

"Makes sense your hair is red then." I felt myself blush at that silly joke. "Yes, I think it suits me just right" I said spinning. We both laughed and I saw Jason smiling from where he was speaking with two cute gentlemen. "You know Jason?" She said following my gaze.

"Yeah, we recently became acquaintances," I replied.

Alyssa gazed at me "Yeah, he has a good taste, follow me, I'll introduce you to some people." I followed her; Jason gave me a thumbs up on my way there. I followed Alyssa to a back room where there were several people sitting and talking while some jazz music served as background music.

I was captivated by a girl wearing a short red dress with pink short hair, she was talking with a guy next to her who matched her beauty, blue eyes, and long brown hair. He was wearing a blue blazer and some gray chinos, with a nice pair of black dressing shoes. This felt like a VIP area and I was just cinderella faking to be a princess for a night.

"Hey everybody this is…." Alyssa looked at me blank I almost turned around and left the room, but I was already here.

"Ruby," I said giving a silly courtesy which caused some smiles from the group. "Ruby this is everyone, you want anything to drink?" She asked pointing at my empty glass.

"Sure," She was off before I could say anything, leaving me alone, again.

"Ruby…, right?" Said the pink-haired girl giving me a warm smile.

"Yes, your hair looks…" I stopped awkwardly as I didn't know how to describe how pretty it looked.

"Pink and yours red, I'm Sheila."

"Yeah, that" I wanted the land to swallow me entirely.

"It's ok, and what brings you here Ruby?" She moved a flock of my hair that was covering my face.

I felt my neck burning up at her touch. "I came with Jason," She didn't pretend to be surprised.

"Yes, he is a good friend of mine as well as my boyfriend Jame there," She pointed at the good-looking boy who was sitting next to her.

"You make a good couple," I complimented her and she smiled boldly.

"Thanks, so do you" That took me off guard, and luckily Alyssa arrived handing me a big glass.

"What did I miss?" She asked as she interrupted our conversation. "Not much, just getting to know our new friend," She said smiling and winking at me before sitting next to her luxurious boyfriend who she gave a kiss on the cheek. I swore she whispered something as he gazed at me, but probably it was all part of my imagination. Alysa kept saying something but I wasn't paying attention, I saw Jason with a couple of friends not far from where I was. He gave me a weird sign wit his brow, I gave him a quick smile and he went back to talking with his friends.

"So… what brings you here, looking for anything in particular?" Alyssa stood next to me.

"I don't know, I have never been one to join these types of meetings before, so honestly I don't know what to expect."

"I see, well just keep an open mind, you can have a good time, now excuse me" she said and dissappeared with a girl who had been staring at her for a while.

I walked around for what felt like forever looking for a bathroom and finally found one in the far end hall. I left my glass in the table outside. I locked myself in one of the bathrooms. Checking at my makeup and hair when the locked door opened. I looked and there she was with her pink hair and red tight dress.

"Ha! Just who I was looking for!" She said before taking a step towards me. Quickly she grabbed me by the back of my neck and pulled me into her locking our lips together, she tasted like cherry and wine with her soft lips and her tongue playing with mine as she kissed me. Her hands touched my tighs and they went up slowly which made my chest heat up, she pushed me to the wall where she turned me, now facing the wall as she left a trace of kisses in my neck and back.

I could smell her sweet cologne and feel her breath on my back which gave me goosebumps. She inserted a warm hand between my tighs, I held a moan as she bit my neck. She flipped me me and kissed me again.

"Do you want me to…?" She lingered on the last word as she touched my tighs.
"Please," I begged and she entered her warm fingers in my mouth which I salivated, and then she lowered them, shoving them in. She knew exactly where to go.

I couldn't keep still; my legs were trembling, the pleasure was taking over me. I felt her perfectly fitting fingers roam in my inner side. I started to moan but she silenced my mouth by kissing me as she slowly pushed inside, making me groan even louder. Smiling she pulled out and made me lick her fingers, tasting myself. Her lips reached mine again, trying to get a taste of me. I was so wet and my legs were still shivering.

"Good girl." She took a napkin, drying her hands. "I'll see you later red Ruby," she said as she exited the bathroom.

I was left there with a tingling sensation all over my body, and my heart slowly calming. Someone stumbled inside the bathroom accompanied and they halt when they saw me. "Don't worry about me, I was leaving." I let them have the bathroom, as I walked out embarrassed but excited, I noticed my glass wasn't there anymore, I couldn't recall how long was I in there.

Jason was standing with some guys and gestured me to go over. "There you are," Ruby this is Liam," he said introducing me to a washed blond with deep black sparkling eyes, he was drooling for Jason.

"Nice to meet you Ruby," He said kissing my hand.

"A gentleman, I like him" I encouraged Jason who laughed.

"Saw pink girl following you earlier" He whispered on my ear, and I felt my whole face was scarlet red. I coughed even though I wasn't drinking anything. "That couple is Fuego" He said mocking and doing a weird gesture with his hands, pink hair walked to the bar with someone but I couldn't see with whom.

"I was telling Liam that this is your first meeting"

"Indeed, very few join in these days, if not by a royal member," Liam said flirting with Jason.

"Excuse me for a second guys, Ruby I leave you in good company, Liam, take care of her."

Liam looked around and we both focused on the pink-hair who seemed to be flirting with a guy.

"She seems to know everyone," Ruby asked,

"Yeah, she knows her way around everyone, its hard to say no to them," He said pointing at her boy who was talking with Jason now.

"I see," Ruby held Liam's shoulder, she wasn't sure if she was supposed to, but it felt right. They both stared at them for a second, until someone came and whispered on Liam's ear, his ears blushing, he gave Ruby a nod and left with a Latin looking guy.

Chapter 4

It was hard to make someone stick around in this place, Ruby felt a little exposed all alone, in the middle of the living room. Jason was too focused on talking with James, and they both seemed to be enjoying themselves. She caught Sheila looking at her and smiling. She smiled back and then someone else stood in front of her, "Hello there, I feel like I've seen you," said a familiar voice.

Ruby looked up and noticed a frequent customer at the bar she worked at during the weekends. "Well, I have three jobs so probably here or there," she mocked as he scanned her.

"Perhaps, I'm Malcolm and this is Fiona," said the thirty-some looking guy with a girl that didn't seem to be enjoying herself. "What brings you here?" He said gazing at her boobs.

"The regular, seductive friend and an open mind," She said and saw Alyssa alone, "If you excuse me, have a great night guys." Ruby walked out as soon as she could, that started to feel completely awkward and Alyssa felt like the perfect getaway.

She joined Alyssa, and then some more people joined them. They talked and drank, someone passed appetizers around and Ruby picked some. It was supposed to be a party solely to meet sexual partners, but everyone seemed so chill that she didn't mind making some potential friends, no one was going to get harmed. Also, she had a shy part to her, walking up to strangers in a fancy party and asking them for sex felt impossible to her. She did catch some people staring at her and sometimes she smiled at them while others she pretended not to notice by laughing too loud or looking in another direction, someone she couldn't stop staring at was Sheila and her boyfriend who wasn't with Jason right now.

Time flew and people were leaving or going somewhere private, the place had many rooms and many were occupied. Ruby saw Jason leave with Sheila's boyfriend and she was talking with a girl and guy, she kissed both of them on the lips before walking away. Ruby pretended to be paying attention to the conversation happening in front of her as she felt Sheilas's gaze on the back of her neck.

"How are you all doing? May I take this pretty girl away from you for a moment," She said before pulling Ruby away. "What are you doing, want to join me upstairs?" She said and Ruby's heart jumped at that invitation. "I'd love to," Ruby said following Sheila's steps, upstairs and beyond.

Ruby saw a couple of people kissing each other, some walking in and out of rooms, the people gathering to drink were less than the ones who were probably messing around. She hadn't come with that mindset to this place, but she didn't even know what she was getting herself into. She just decided to agree to a nice guy who she met who was the same guy who always went with different dates to the bar, so yeah she should've known better. Now she was following a pink-haired girl to an unknown place, she didn't know what she was going to find, but honestly. She felt ready, nervous, but ready.

Sheila opened a set of double rooms, there was a group of people some naked and some in underwear, a guy fucking with another guy as a girl rimmed him, a couple of girls kissing each other and one of them sitting on top of a guy. The room filled with sweat, smelling like sex and lit candles. Sheila turned and kept walking, crossing a set of big curtains and behind them was a king bed and two guys shirtless kissing each other. She noticed Jason and James, kissing in a passionate, yet eager way. Their lips and chest clashing. She felt like she wasn't supposed to watch that, but then James noticed Ruby there and brought himself to Sheila who he kissed with something more than just lust. He took a deep look at Ruby who he pulled closer and kissed, his beard made her skin tickle but his kisses were firm and it both felt and tasted good, just as she had imagined.

The room was filled with a sensual aroma, Ruby started to feel funny, had someone poured something in her drink, were the candles filled with something? A moment later she was kissing the shirtless James and next they were all just in underwear. She noticed a nice eagle tattoo on James' chest and a butterfly on Sheila's. Jason walked towards her, smiling. "Relax Princess and don't forget to have a good time," He said before kissing her slowly, at first, she felt weird by kissing Jason. He grabbed her ass tightly, kissing her neck passionately, making his way to her breasts which he caressed with both hands as he looked at her. Sheila joined him and they kissed Ruby as they both grabbed her chest, making Ruby hold a moan by biting her lips. James hugged her from behind, kissing the side of her neck and caressing her shoulders. He left a tray of kisses as he touched her abdomen.

He freed her breasts and held them on his hands as he kissed her neck, making her moan. Both Jason and Sheila knelt in front of her, licking her breasts, one on each side. Ruby was trying to contain herself, but their touch, their tounges on her nipples was making it harder and harder to control herself. Sheila nib on her nipple which freed a loud cry, she looked at Ruby with lust painted all over her face and kissed her. Bringing with her that sweet taste of her kisses and her delicate but firm touch.

Now both boys were all over her chest. Sheila had her tongue inside of Ruby's mouth and played with her finger around Ruby's clit, she made slow circles making Ruby gasp as she kept tempting her. Sheila then shoved all of her fingers all the way as Ruby started crying, James kissed her neck and Jason licked her breasts. She was being overwhelmed by sensation, touch, smell. She couldn't control her body as it shuddered. Kissing, licking, biting, fingering. There wasn't a part of her body left unattended.

They were everywhere. Suddenly, Ruby felt something hard pushing against her bottom! It was James' dick rubbing between her butt cheeks. She became more aware of her body, of what she felt, every kiss, every touch felt like stars exploding on her body, making her shiver all around. She was enjoying herself and someone blew on her cherry then lick around it and slowly caressed it, pulling her clit slowly, which brought her to tears. They kept playing with her, abusing her, using her, she was tied to them, her body shivering and the feels were too much. She felt the heat intensifying on her chest as they kept caressing her in all the right places. Jason kissed her neck and whispered "let go baby, enjoy it" As if by command she felt her orgasm approaching, from the kissing, licking, touching and pulling. Pleasure traveled around her body like sparks, commotion with every touch.

Ruby started to moan louder and louder, they all kept going at the same rhythm, her heartbeat racing. They increased their speed, she felt herself go in an explosion of color with a big cry.

And they kept going, Jason started to kiss James and Sheila was in between them. Engulfing herself with Jason's meat as they kissed each other. Ruby stared at them and she felt her temperature rise slowly again.

She had just started, but she wanted to watch them now.

James knelt and he and Sheila licked this other guy's, Rafael's hard hairy cock, as they kissed each other, licking him from both sides, their tongues colliding. Jason moaned as he watched them play with him. Then someone entered their room, he had just a hat, black dressing pants and a tie, he was shirtless. Had he arrived shirtless or did he leave his shirt somewhere else?

He joined Jason from behind and kissed him, he bit his neck as Sheila and James still filled themselves with his meat. The new arrival whispered something on his neck and Jason nodded, the newcomer lowered himself to Jason's bottom and started to lick and bite his cheeks, groaning Jason kept pushing back, feeding him his behind as the guy held his buttcheeks open and spread his tongue all around.

Jason started moaning louder, and they kept playing with him. Then the newcomer raised to his mouth and kissed him passionately, Ruby started to touch herself as she enjoyed the show. But Sheila joined her and sat at her side, and kissed her. The boys kept playing and now Jason started to rim James' trimmed butt. They were a nice wrecking train, Jason eating James behind as James sucked on the newcomer's big meat. Sheila licked Ruby's nipple and bit on it as she looked up and licked her ear.

Ruby was playing with herself, feeling her wetness arise and Sheila held her hand placing it carefully on top of her wet cunt, Ruby touched her and licked her, she lowered herself and opened her legs eating her up. Sheila moaned as Ruby made her way into her cherry, her smell, her taste was sweet and delicious. She was wet which turned Ruby on, and then she felt someone behind her, a loud sharp spank leaving a buzzing sensation on her right cheek, followed by another on the left.

She was wet from before and ready as she devoured Sheila's cherry, and then someone entered her, she felt it making its way first slowly inside and then a deep, powerful trust making her boobs move, Sheila lowered herself now lying below Ruby, as James fucked her, holding onto her waist and looking at Sheila playing with herself as Ruby kissed her neck and licked her nipples. She could feel her hands as she moved in circles, pleasing herself. She heard Jason moaning as he entered James who gave another hard-thrust inside of Ruby's wet cunt, making her cry out loud.

"Fuck," James screamed.

"Harder," Jason told the newcomer who was banging him from behind as he fucked Jason who was kneeling behind Ruby, fucking her. It looked like a renascent painting, their bodies covered in sweat, connected by the flesh.

Ruby played with Sheila's breasts as she played with herself, approaching her climax. James increased his speed and Jason pulled out of him, whispering something in his ear. Something about letting him enjoy freely of Ruby's. Then she felt something slippery penetrate her bottom. James shoved his dick covered in her own juices straight up her ass. Ruby wasn't prepared for this and it was overwhelming, she let out a long cry.

Slowly James made his way in, caressing ruby's back and ass, he started thrusting harder and faster. Quickly, she felt her inside falling apart and her climax claiming her. She couldn't think no more, as she was laying down there on all fours Sheila started to finger her near oozing clit while still masturbating herself. Taking it in both her ass and pussy she was felt completely at their mercy. Ruby closed her eyes putting her head against the padding, trying to hold out the moans. Couple more strokes, his dick was filling her ass fully. James felt her ass encircling and pulling his dick deeper.

"Ahh, Fuck yes! James shouted.

She heard James groan and with two more pushes, she felt his cum inside, his warmness filling her, Sheila also came in a nice warm squirt which reached Ruby's breasts and stomach. Ruby started to lick Sheila and as she licked her, Jason shoved his hard dick inside Ruby's pussy. He kept fucking her, it wasn't slow or sensual, he was in fact pounding himself as quick and hard as he possibly could. Ruby was being moved around each time his dick hit her vaginal wall, slamming against her butt cheeks. It allowed Ruby to tongue Sheila deep in steady intervals and soon enough she felt the explosion on her face as she reached that colorful orgasm once again, squirting all over Ruby's face. By the same time, Jason groaned and pulled his dick out, spraying Ruby's cheeks all the way to her lower back.

The afterward felt awkward, but they all kissed, touched each other, and kept talking. But for some reason, ruby felt dirty in many different ways, they all gathered their belongings. Sheila kissed her before leaving and so did James. Everyone seemed to greet with a peek. "I guess I'll see you around," Sheila whispered as they departed ways in the parking lot. Ruby followed Jason to his car and she saw them get on theirs and leave.

"How do you feel?" Jason asked as he drove around.

"Honestly, dirty." She said laughing at herself.

"We quite literally are" he said joining her laugh. "You hungry?"

Epilogue

They reached his apartment faster than she could've thought. Jason told there is a shower at the end of the hall, there are towels and a robe she could change into that while you are here, "or even better, nothing" He said giving her a seductive smile.

Ruby entered this massive shower, which could fit probably an orgy in, perhaps it already had she thought to herself. She needed to leave those thoughts out of her head. The warm water felt easing as it touched every part of her still sensitive body, she still could feel them everywhere, the shower wasn't helping. She heard some noise in the background and turned the shower a bit higher, Jason had opened the door, silently he sneaked up behind her. He slapped Ruby's ass, making her wince. Ruby seemed to be daydreaming as he kissed her neck.

"Are you OK?" he asked with a warm tone to his voice.

"Yes, of course" she managed to say as he kissed her back and caressed her ass with his hardness.

The shower was filled with steam warm water as he pushed Ruby to the shower wall, entering her, filling her. He felt different than James did, he was thicker and it hit right on her spot. She touched herself as he thrust in and out of her. Kissing her neck as he started to pound Ruby's swollen cunt faster.

"Yes baby, please don't stop!" Ruby screamed and she felt his hold tighten on her waist. Jason held onto her waist so tight it was compressing her hips, she was going to get bruises from this night, but she couldn't care less.

He kept shoving himself in until he filled her with his seed. He hugged her and washed her hair under the shower.

"This was fun, did you have fun, Scarlett?" He said still playing with her name, "Yes, I did" Her cheeks blushing not letting her lie about it. It was an overwhelming yes, she felt a little dirty but now with his company she felt better.

"I have an extra room, if you want to move in, I think we could become great friends in the long run, Ruby in shock stuttered her reply. "Really? Here? I'd love to."

Jason smiled at her and left a quick kiss on her hand. "Well so it's settled My Scarlett," he lifted a glass of wine, smiled at her, and clinked their glasses together. "To living, he said smiling at her.

"To living," Ruby replied and she knew her adventure had just begun...